1 – 168

T 7590

D0574625

E
Ros

Ross, Katharine
The little ballerina

The Little Ballerina

By Katharine Ross

Illustrated by Heidi Petach

A Random House PICTUREBACK®

Random House New York

Text copyright © 1996 by Random House, Inc. Illustrations copyright © 1996 by Heidi Petach.
Published in the United States by Random House, Inc., New York, and simultaneously in Canada
by Random House of Canada Limited, Toronto.

Library of Congress Cataloging-in-Publication Data
Ross, Katharine. The little ballerina / by Katharine Ross.   p.   cm.—(A Pictureback book)
SUMMARY: The Little Ballerina practices hard with the others in her class and experiences the thrill
of a big dance recital.   ISBN: 0-679-84915-7 (trade)   [1. Ballet dancing—Fiction.]   I. Title.
PZ7.R719693Le   1994   [E]—dc20   92-42093

Manufactured in the United States of America   10 9 8 7 6 5 4 3 2 1

17168

Once upon a time there was a Little Ballerina.

The Little Ballerina had a suitcase that looked like a little pink drum. When the children on the bus saw that little pink case, they knew it was ballet day.

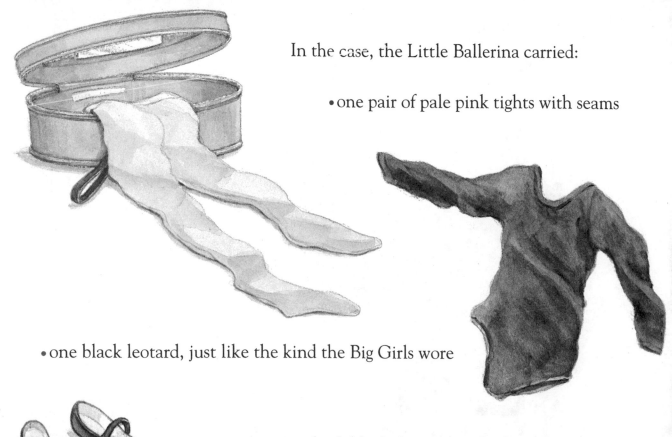

In the case, the Little Ballerina carried:

• one pair of pale pink tights with seams

• one black leotard, just like the kind the Big Girls wore

• one pair of soft black slippers, with elastic bands that she had sewed on herself

• talcum powder—one shake for each slipper

• one fat rubber band and four bobby pins to put her hair up into an almost-bun

First position,   second position,   third position,

fourth…

In the playground, the Little Ballerina stood by the jungle gym and practiced moving her arms and feet in the five basic ballet positions.

"Come play!" her friends begged, but…

...second position, third position, fourth position, fifth.

The Little Ballerina wouldn't play today. She had to practice, for tomorrow was the Big Recital! She practiced until the bell rang and recess was over.

After school, the Little Ballerina ran all the way to the big white house on Sycamore Street where Mamzelle taught ballet. Mamzelle was what the girls called their ballet teacher.

Down in the basement the girls all changed together.

The hooks down low were for the little girls.

The hooks up high were for the Big Girls.

"Someday," said the Little Ballerina, looking up at the hooks, "I'll hang my clothes up there."

She put her hair up in an almost-bun after dressing as quickly as she could.

Skipping every other step, she ran upstairs to peek in the window at the biggest girls. They were crowding around Mamzelle, smiling at her and clapping. Everyone knew what that meant: "Thank you, Mamzelle, for a class well taught." The Little Ballerina knew—as everyone else knew too—that little girls didn't clap for Mamzelle, they curtsied.

Mamzelle started class at the *barre* (bahr), the long handrail used for balancing that ran all the way down one side of the room, along a wall of mirrors. First, *pliés* (plee-AYS), soft and graceful. *Plié* in French refers to a movement in which the knees are bent while the back is held straight.

"Breathe," said Mamzelle. "Breathe, little girls!" And
the Little Ballerina remembered to breathe. It was hard
not to hold her breath when she was doing something so
very difficult.

Frappés (fra-PAYS) came next.

"Yummy frappés" the Little Ballerina liked to call them, because the word reminded her of a special milk shake her aunt had treated her to in Boston. She did frappés by beating her foot lightly against the inside of her ankle.

"Concentrate!" Mamzelle told them again and again.

"Stop squinching those toes!" Mamzelle said to the Little Ballerina.

"Squinching" was a word Mamzelle had learned from her girls. Squinching happened when her girls concentrated a little *too* hard.

And then, in an order so rapid that the Little Ballerina's head began to swim, Mamzelle had them do:

tendus (tahn-DOOS)　　　　　　　　　and *piqués* (pee-KAYS).

Mamzelle had them do:

petits battements (puh-TEE bat-MAHNT)

and *grands battements* (grahnd bat-MAHNT).

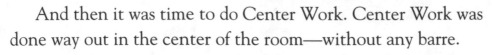

And then it was time to do Center Work. Center Work was done way out in the center of the room—without any barre.

The girls spread out, arm's length apart, three deep, littlest ones up front. The bigger girls in back tried to hide themselves behind the littler ones, but Mamzelle always said to them: "Girls, don't you know you cannot hide in a room full of mirrors?"

They started with an *adagio* (uh-DAHJ-ee-o). *Adagio* means slow. It was hard at first not to lose her balance, but the Little Ballerina knew how important it was to learn to balance— without any barre.

Tour (toor) is a French word that means a turn. The tour, or *pirouette* (pir-ooh-ET), was the hardest step of all. To turn round and round without ever getting dizzy was something the Little Ballerina still had to learn. She picked a spot to stare at with all her might and never took her eyes off it. The spot helped her to feel as if only her body were turning while her head stood stock-still. The head was the part that got dizzy. The Little Ballerina's favorite spot was an old paint smear on the floor that looked like a yellow rose.

After class, the Little Ballerina quickly ran up
and curtsied for Mamzelle.

"I'm ready, Mamzelle. For tomorrow, Mamzelle."

"Be at the Big Auditorium at five o'clock sharp
and don't forget your costume, Little Ballerina."

The Little Ballerina nodded and smiled.
Tomorrow was the Big Recital.

That night, when the sky was velvety black and the stars shone like diamonds, the Little Ballerina slept and dreamed she was a Princess who danced on her toes—without ever getting dizzy.

The Princess danced round and round, holding a spindle in her hand. The spindle was a gift from the Wicked Fairy, who hadn't been invited to her christening—sixteen long years ago.

The princess pricked her finger on the spindle and fell dead. But the Lilac Fairy—who *had* been invited to the christening—cast a spell that made the Princess sleep instead.

She slept on and on, in a castle overgrown with briers. She slept a hundred years or more. Until one day, a handsome Prince followed the Lilac Fairy through the brambles to the bed where the Princess lay sleeping. He kissed her on the lips and she awoke, and that very day they were married.

They danced a *pas de deux* (pah de DUH), a dance for two persons. In the corps were all the fairies who had been at her christening. The Lilac Fairy, the Fountain Fairy, and the Fairies of the Crystal and the Glade. Even the Sunbeam Fairy was there, and for a few moments she danced a little dance all by herself in the center of the palace hall. And then the whole company danced together in a colorful swirl until…

...the Little Ballerina woke up.

She jumped out of bed and said with a cry,
"Today is Recital Day!"

That night, in the dressing room of the Big Auditorium, the Little Ballerina got dressed. Her mother helped put on green eye shadow, pink blush, red lipstick, and orange sunrays shooting out from her eyebrows. The Little Ballerina was a sunbeam!

On her hair there was hair spray to hold her almost-bun together and a big orange headdress made of feathers that bobbed and waved when she moved.

The mothers—and a few fathers—
had made the costumes. They were made
of wonderful stuff: taffeta and satin, silk
and gauze—all dyed in glorious colors.
The mothers—and a few fathers—had
dyed the girls' tights and leotards to
match their costumes.

Mamzelle came backstage and visited her girls.
"Remember to breathe, little girls," she said.
The Little Ballerina nodded. "Yes, Mamzelle," she whispered.
How her heart fluttered!

Then the music began and the curtain rang up and the
Dance of the Sunbeams began. The Little Ballerina danced
the steps of the dance as if she'd known them always, as if
she'd learned them in a dream.

Afterward, her father and mother came backstage and gave her flowers.

She curtsied and said: "Did you see when I itched my nose?"

"Never," said her father. "Sunbeams don't have noses."

Her parents asked her to choose a place to have dinner, any place in town.

"The Hot Shop, please," the Little Ballerina said, "for a cheeseburger and a chocolate shake!"

At the Hot Shop, the Little Ballerina looked around and blinked and yawned and stretched. The other people there stared and smiled at the Little Ballerina in her Sunbeam costume. She smiled back sleepily.

In the car riding home, the Little Ballerina wondered if she'd ever been up this late before. And her head grew heavy as someone whispered, "Go to sleep, Little Ballerina, and rest."